A HEART FULL OF WORDS

WORDS

AN ENSEMBLE OF RIVETING SHORT STORIES

Titilayo Obasanya

A HEART FULL OF WORDS: an ensemble of riveting short stories.

A Heart Full of Words is a compilation of short stories that explores themes of love, loss, faith, identity, and the complexities of the human experience in a compelling narrative style.

The Girl My Father Never Wanted

When Ifeyinwa Okoye was born, her father, a junior-ranking police officer, vowed he would not use his hard-earned money to put her through school, a decree that did not apply to her brothers. Nevertheless, for many years, she desired nothing more than to be her father's favourite. She wanted to call him Nna, as her brothers did with affection. But she called him Sir. That was all that she could muster, even when her heart tried to push away the ocean of hatred she had for him. 'The Girl My Father Never Wanted' is a poignant account of Ifeyinwa's struggle to hold onto threads of hope amid bitterness, pain, and seemingly unending chaos.

Prisoner of Guilt

Moshood Adebayo is the Strategic and Partnerships Manager (EMEA) at Hemads Oil and Gas. He lost his wife, Amy, five years ago and could not move on even though he sought closure. His colleague, Justin Jones, recommended therapy when he noticed Moshood's performance at work was declining. During a session with Dr Paula Wilson, Moshood revealed the root cause of his intermittent illness when he let out a shockingly terrible secret.

Miracles Everywhere

Pastor Josh and his wife, Pastor Anna, co-founded a multicultural, non-denominational church to be a beacon of hope for teens and young adults in their community. Pastor Anna reckoned the Gospel message was just what their borough needed to restore oneness and love after a mass brawl involving two hundred people. After eight months, the church membership snowballed, and it became notable for remarkable miracles. Even Pastor Josh's son was said to have received a touch from heaven and healed of a rare genetic disorder. Or was he not? 'Miracles Everywhere' is a thought-provoking story that will make you question the motive and authenticity of your faith.

The Girl My Father Never Wanted

Loud applause filled the room as Ifeyinwa walked gracefully across the stage. It was so well polished that she saw her face reflected in the archaic wood. Everything in the auditorium looked perfect—the chandeliers, the early spring flowers carefully arranged in crystal vases at the edge of the stage. In their pristine ceremonial purple gowns with golden tassels hanging down from the sides of their caps, the graduating students joyously awaited the start of the ceremony, cheering as Ifeyinwa walked up to the podium. She looked radiant, but her glow stemmed neither from the colourful painted glass on the ceiling above her nor from the sun rays piercing the light blue clouds. It was a glow from within that lit up her entire body, a glow that erupted from the rich tapestry of deep matters of the heart.

"Thank you. Thank you. Thank you." Ifeyinwa's voice echoed through the auditorium as a captivating smile formed across her lips.

A student yelled from the back of the room, "I love you!"

"I love you too," Ifeyinwa giggled, her dangling freshwater pearl earrings swaying to the rhythm of her laughter. "I love you more." Then, she turned to the professors and senior academic staff on stage. "Thank you for your warm welcome and kind invitation, Professor

Clark," she began. "What a privilege to share this remarkable day with Frank Edison University."

The Progressive National Education Board (PNEB) recognised Frank Edison University as the pioneer of social justice studies when they published a research-based framework that universities worldwide have since adopted as the single source of truth to evaluate, correct, and embrace institutional practices meant to eliminate inequality. Frank Edison University's Academy for Social Justice had indeed earned a name amongst its peers, and to celebrate this incredible milestone on graduation day, the Board of Directors decided it was appropriate to host a speaker with experiential knowledge of social justice—Ifeyinwa Okoye.

Ifeyinwa adjusted the papers she had carefully placed on the podium, feeling the intense gazes of the students. She was an unassuming speaker known for her storytelling, which left her listeners still deciding about their emotional response to her message. Some cried, some screamed and laughed, and many were often sombre and reflective.

"Oh, a side note," she continued, "I am usually not as tall as I am today. Thank you for the extra elevated stage." Then she whispered, "Marvellous things often come in small sizes—five foot two inches." The crowd roared with laughter.

She took a sip of water and adjusted her glasses. When she had to appear in public, she always wore her favourite pair, black plastic frames with big, round lenses, gold temples, and nose bridge.

"Congratulations to the class of 2016! You look delighted, relieved, maybe a little too joyful?" She paused for the joke to sink in. "Happy! Yes, happy is the word. You look happy, and indeed, you should be happy. You should be proud of your achievements, your parents, guardians and support system. You should be proud of your late nights and early mornings; those long caffeine-fueled days served you well, and if you are like me, an extra hot latte was my energy booster in grad school." She looked at her notes and continued. "At graduation ceremonies, it is often easy to forget the entire journey of your study, especially if you don't consider the smaller, seemingly inconsequential memories that, taken together, got you to where you are today. Today, I'd like to remind you to be grateful—grateful for the things you couldn't control that worked out in your favour, grateful for the people who controlled things that you could not control and ensured it all worked out in your favour, and grateful for the things you had complete control over and followed through on. It is impossible to truly appreciate what one has, to be grateful in the purest way, if you have never considered what your story could have been. So, I will share my story with you.

My mother had me at forty-four weeks, which I believe is symbolic of my life's journey. She held me in her womb longer than necessary as if she knew she wouldn't have enough chances to carry me in her arms after I was born. She passed away just five years after my birth, at the age of thirty-six. There were six of us when she died—"five boys and Ifeyinwa." That's how my father introduced us to people.

My mother was twenty-five years old when she married my father, and although she looked older than her age, childbearing aged her even more, making her look drawn and worn. She always cooked, cleaned, ensured everyone was okay, and did most of the household chores herself. My brothers were young and could only help so much. I came six years later, on her thirty-first birthday, when resources were intentionally scarce. My father had vowed that he would never pay my tuition because he did not plan on having another child. He said his savings had been pre-allocated to more critical projects like building a retirement home in Ikot Abasi, one of the thirty-one local government areas of Akwa-Ibom State in Nigeria, and realising his lifetime dream of becoming a cassava farmer. He also viewed female education as a complete waste of time and felt that women should not be allowed too much independence lest they become proud and disrespectful to their husbands. Yes, I know; he was ignorant and misogynistic.

Sadly, my mother could not step in to support me because she was a housewife who relied on him for literally everything. Besides, how much did a junior-ranking police officer earn? I would argue it wasn't enough to care for a family of four, let alone a family of eight.

Unsurprisingly, the boys were exempt from this austerity, attending the local public school in their pristine school uniforms, which they kept neat all day. For years, I wanted to be like my brothers, to speak and walk as confidently as they did, and to participate in their chatter about what they would become when they were older—a banker, a scientist, an engineer, a teacher, and a footballer.

I longed for an education, and for this reason, I wanted to be my father's favourite and to be loved by Nna, which means father in the Igbo language, as the boys called him affectionately. I called him Sir. That was the most I could muster. Even when my heart tried to push away my hatred for him, "Sir" was all I could manage.

Exactly three days after my mother passed, Sir called me to the storage room and ordered me to clean up. I asked if Chinedu, my eldest brother, could help me with the heavy boxes. I told him my tiny hands could only sweep and clean the dirty furniture. I was, after all, only five years old. To my surprise, Sir, who stood six foot three inches and whose palm was the size of a Thaumatococcus daniellii leaf that mother occasionally used for wrapping a bean pudding before steaming it, responded with a slap. My head must have spun around in circles before my small frame landed on the terrazzo floor.

This incident was the beginning of many more beatings. Sir's weapon of choice was his black leather police belt, the same one he made me polish meticulously every Saturday evening while my brothers played in the yard. Sir was as generous with his verbal abuse as he was with his physical. What was my offence, one might ask? I don't know. He often said I was too ambitious. Over the years, my once-fragile heart toughened, and I hated Sir more and more.

Most days, while my brothers were at school, I selected a few of their old books and read them until I fell asleep. At other times, I set up a makeshift classroom. I'd put up a blackboard, write words and sentences from their English books, and read them aloud a few times until I memorised them.

On Thursday afternoon, July 25, 1986, Sir beckoned 15-year-old me during my home-schooling session. I had just learned the word "hippopotamus." The word sounded very foreign and amusing: H-I-P-P-O-P-O-T-A-M-U-S. I spelled it out loud many times and laughed each time I got it correct until Sir asked me to keep quiet. He pushed his long, skinny fingers against the back of my head a few times, jostling my head forward each time.

"To your room now!" Sir scolded. He followed me there. "Pick up those dirty clothes of yours," he ordered, thrusting a black plastic bag at me. "Put them in this bag and come with me."

Once I'd done as I was told, he marched out of my room and out of our compound. For a moment, I was excited; I thought he had finally agreed to let me spend the weekend at my friend Kike's house. Kike's mum had pressured Sir a few times, but he always said no. As I stepped out of our compound, my heart sank when I eyed our next-door neighbour, Mrs Ebere Chukwu, instead of Kike's mom. She had no children, though each time I asked, she said she hoped to have a little girl like me one day. She even told me she would name her Ifeyinwa—the inquisitive one! Her calm smile felt like my mother's embrace.

Sir looked down at his feet and said to her, "As you know, I have no plans to remarry, but Ifeyinwa needs a mother." He cleared his throat gently while two flies danced around his head. "I discussed this with Ifeyinwa, and she is happy to go with you to Abia State. My sons think it is a wonderful idea." He choked between his words, pretending to be emotional.

I felt my world shatter. *Where is Abia State?* I wondered. *What am I going to do there? What could I have done to deserve this? Was it because I look like my mother, and I reminded him of her demise? Was it because I was the child they never planned to have? The girl he never wanted? Am I an adopted child?* My eyes opened wide as the tiny muscles under my arms contracted, and all at once, the numbered hairs on my arms stood on end, creating goosebumps. I could not manage a word out of my mouth. Even today, I wonder if that reaction was out of fear of Sir's retribution or disbelief that I would never see my brothers again. I was sure my brothers did not know Sir had put a permanent divide between us, and I could only imagine what he would say to them once I was gone.

Sir looked at me from the corner of his eye, but then, quick as a flashing light, he looked away just as I was about to summon the courage to ask why he had been so cruel towards me.

"Thank you for your love, Madam," he said as he traced his steps back to his compound. I reached out my arms as if to pull him back, but he slammed the gate.

Mrs Ebere Chukwu beckoned to her husband, Reverend Father Mark Chukwu, and they both held me close as I wailed. Catholics recently assigned to support foreign missionaries in Abia State, they were kind-hearted and compassionate, though noticeably reserved, and I was inconsolable. Unbeknownst to me, Sir had timed my departure carefully. As soon as he left, the Chukwus loaded their trunk with their luggage, and off we went to a place they called an orphanage.

What is an orphanage? I wondered. "It is called St. Margaret Orphanage," Mrs Chukwu said. It felt like she had read my thoughts. "The hostel is only a fifteen-minute walk from our new home at the Missionary Lodge," she noted, promising to visit me often. "You will love it there. We wouldn't have accepted your father's request to help you find a home if we didn't think it was a good place for you. We have helped so many girls like you find new life at the orphanage. For us, it is a home away from home. And your father said he and your brothers will visit you once you are settled."

I smiled as I thought of my oldest sibling, Chinedu. He had told me about his dream of going away to boarding school for his senior secondary schooling because they had really lovely hostels. But I didn't believe anything that Mrs Chukwu was telling me. I was afraid.

It started to rain heavily. First came a loud clap, then a rumble. I covered my ears tightly as I dove under Mrs Chukwu's seat. The wipers moved fast but not fast enough to keep the buckets of water off the windshield. My stomach churned. I had eaten no solid meal since last night, thanks to Sir's punishment. He only allowed me to drink water and lemongrass tea for breakfast whenever I read too long, an unpardonable offence.

After two hours, Reverend Father Mark slowed the vehicle down, signalled left, and drove into the driveway of what looked like the biggest mansion I had ever seen. It was picturesque, nestled in the middle of an immaculate garden. My eyes darted from one detail to another as I tried to soak everything in quickly. I raced out of the car when he brought the vehicle to a stop right in front of the orphanage's entrance. With trembling hands, I opened the door and saw a long hallway lined with doors on both sides. My imagination soared! *Is this my new home?*

I opened each door as I walked down the hallway.

Unlike back home, the rooms were super clean and spacious, and each had an inexplicable presence, inviting me in to explore. But I kept walking—until I noticed a stairway on my left. I was about to wander up the stairs when I heard Mrs Chukwu's voice.

"Ifeyinwa, that's a no-go area," she told me. "Your room is further down the hall."

I ran ahead of Mrs Chukwu until I came to a door with a signpost that read, "Welcome home." I pushed the door open slowly, not sure what to expect. It was enchanting—a room full of toys and books—too many to count. I jumped on the big bed, holding a giant teddy in my arms, tears streaming down my cheeks.

Mrs Chukwu walked in and introduced me to someone she called Sister Emily. Sister Emily was the orphanage manager, but she became so much more to me as time went by; she was my confidant, the shoulder I could lean on anytime, my counsellor, and my teacher.

Stepping into the orphanage that day was a defining moment in my life. I wished my brothers knew where I was. I tried to imagine the lies Sir would have told them, wondering if any of them ever thought to look for me. I was determined then and there to redefine my destiny and author my success story, which I still defined as education, finding freedom and love, even if I was never placed with a new family that would love me unconditionally.

Staying at the orphanage was one of the best things that happened to me. It was decades ago, but it remains an unfaded memory. I learned how to read, write, and be confident yet empathetic. I met many lovely girls, some of whom are still my friends. Over the years, we built a powerful bond that transcended the hostel's walls. St. Margaret Orphanage taught me the most important lesson—that I was enough and did not have to fight to win anyone's approval, not even Sir's. I learned that self-love is the bedrock of accomplishing anything worthwhile in life. Realising this freed my soul, but it did not heal me completely.

Sir was cruel! I need only look at the ugly scars on my wrist from the dry, twisted fig branches he used to flog me countless times to be reminded of his inhumanity. But actually, I see these same scars in a different light today. I see them as an outward reflection of my once-crushed spirit and broken heart.

On my eighteenth birthday, three years after arriving at the orphanage, Sister Emily told me she had found me the perfect home. My new parents walked into my room with cupcakes, sweets, and a little puppy they placed in my arms.

"Her name is Bella," they announced in unison.

I felt her spirit come alive as I held the puppy close to my chest. "Bella was my mother's middle name," I whispered.

They told me they had five girls and had always dreamt of a house full of girls. I was delighted as I rehearsed calling Mr Iheme Dad, Daddy, or Papa. *He will be my hero, and Mrs Iheme, my earthly mother*, I thought to myself. *My mother will smile from heaven. She can now rest in peace, knowing I am in safe hands.*

But their niceness seemed to end as soon as we left the orphanage. Sitting upright with my hands clasped on my thigh in the Iheme's car, which was utterly filthy and saturated with a foul odour, I tried to make small talk, but they ignored me.

"How old is Bella?" I asked.

Mrs Iheme turned sharply to her husband. "Do it now!" she barked.

Mr Iheme slowed the car down before stopping at a busy roadside where street vendors bargained with buyers under the scorching sun. He stretched his arms towards me. "Give her to me now," he ordered, pointing to the dog. He carried Bella in his arms and walked away from the car until I lost sight of him.

When he returned, I asked, "Where is Bella?" Mrs Iheme smiled awkwardly. "Papa sold her in the open market. We don't really like dogs," she shrugged. That was the first red flag. And, perhaps not surprisingly, my first night at the Ihemes' was the most awful experience ever. We arrived at 10:00 p.m. after being on the road for about three hours. I was exhausted but strangely had a little hope left in me for a welcome similar to the one I had received when I arrived at the orphanage. I had imagined how my new sisters would dote over me, as Mrs Iheme had told Sister Emily they couldn't wait to meet the newest member of the family.

In reality, and to my disbelief, the girls did not say a single word to me upon my arrival. Instead, they curtsied and chorused between yawns, "Welcome Papa, welcome Mama." I smiled at each of them, only to be met with stone cold stares before they all turned around and marched into their room like members of a cadet band. It was another red flag, but I made excuses for my new sisters. "Perhaps it's past their bedtime," I whispered to myself as I followed behind them. "Or maybe they did not know I was arriving today."

The Ihemes lived in a small two-bedroom bungalow in Nsukka, Enugu State, Nigeria. Mr and Mrs Iheme slept in the bigger of the two bedrooms, and the girls shared the smaller one. The three youngest girls slept on a queen-sized mattress, while the two eldest had small mattresses by the window. Examining the uneven, cemented floor, I reluctantly took my shoes off and politely asked the older girls to put their mattresses together so that I, too, could have a place to sleep since I was not welcomed with a mattress of my own. They hissed in unison, long enough for me to know not to ask again.

"Dad!" I yelled at the top of my lungs as I stomped out of the room. Mrs Iheme opened the door to her room, and I heard Mr Iheme snoring like a congested Rhino. "obere nwa agbọghọ, *little girl*, take this," she said, giving me a brown handwoven mat and a blanket. "I will buy you a mattress. It is a long day tomorrow; get some sleep now!"

Settled in my makeshift bed, I shut my eyes, but sleep wouldn't come. Suddenly, a lightning bolt revealed tall avocado and guava trees outside the window. The breeze that escorted a heavy downpour was refreshing, but still, I could not rest. *Why me?* The question played itself over and over in my mind. Then, I began to think about my mother. Was there no cure for the deadly worms that Sir said ate up her intestines? I wished I was older before she died. Maybe I would have given her some salty water and cured her. It was not until many years later that I would learn from one of her friends, who I met by happenstance, that she died of ovarian cancer.

The hairs on my legs stood at attention, a reaction to the strong wind that rushed into the cramped bedroom at the break of dawn. From the corners of my sleepy eyes, I could see that all five girls were already up and dressed in tattered blouses with wrappers tied around their waists. Oddly, each carried a rusty metal tray on her head, the kind my mother used to air maize. Looking closely, I spotted roasted and boiled nuts and crushed moringa tea leaves in small transparent plastic bags on the trays.

"It is now time!" Mrs Iheme yelled. "We don't have all day, Ifeyinwa."

I got up at once and rushed to the bathroom. Then she handed me a tray full of nuts and tea leaves, just like the other girls, and did a headcount. "Ada, Amaka, Nneka, Chichi, Mary, and now we have Ifeyinwa." She clapped her hands. "Sooner or later, even more girls will join our association." She looked sternly at me and then continued. "Ifeyinwa, you will be a proud owner of a kiosk at the Bantu Market Square in a few years. I tell the girls all the time that they don't need men or education to become successful market traders. Look at me!" She spun around majestically. "Who would have thought? I came to Enugu State with nothing, but now I own ten kiosks. And girls just like you, who received adequate training, are proud franchise owners. They pay me a monthly fee and ten per cent commission on sales for five years, which is their way of saying thank you for training them."

It was at that point that I realised the Ihemes were child traffickers! None of the girls were their biological children.

"Ifeyinwa! Ifeyinwa!!" Mrs Iheme called out, jerking me back to life and handing me a small scarf, which she instructed me to roll into a ball. It was meant to cushion my head from the friction and heat of the tray when the sun came out in its full glory.

I was lucky. My thick, full hair was made into cornrows, giving me an added layer of protection. Looking at the other girls, I noticed they all had the same short haircut. I hoped I wouldn't have to cut my hair to match theirs.

But it was as if Mrs Iheme knew exactly what I was thinking. "We need to give you a cut," she said right then and there; "the tray won't sit properly with your cornrows."

At that moment, I had a quick flashback to one of the stories Sister Emily told us at the orphanage one Friday night. It was a story about a boy who was haunted in his dreams by a farmer after he lost the farmer's cocoa seeds on a school excursion. So, I said that my dead mother would haunt her if she dared to give me a haircut. She looked at me in disbelief, but I could tell she was afraid. She shrugged and said, "You don't need a haircut."

We started at 5:30 a.m. and closed for the day at 6:30 p.m., hawking on street corners and highways. My tender feet could not move as fast as the other girls, but I kept pushing, walking through one roadside at a time. Our mission was to sell all our merchandise and earn some proceeds from the sale for a job well done.

Five years at the Ihemes' seemed like ten years. It was the same routine day in and day out except on Saturdays and Sundays, where we were allowed some time to rest and recover.

I continued to desire an education, as I defined success as being educated. That was all I wanted. However, I soon realised that success takes time and often comes at a hefty price. I saved all the money I earned until it was enough to pay my bus fare and sustain me for a few months, and finally, on Christmas Eve 1994, I summoned enough courage to leave the Iheme's house, having carefully planned my escape.

It was midnight, and the girls were fast asleep when I picked up my backpack, which I had hidden behind the cane chair in the living room, climbed out of the window, and began my walk to freedom. It was a long walk to the bus garage, where I boarded a bus to Lagos State.

I woke up to the noise of what I thought could easily be an army of a thousand traders. We were in Yaba, Lagos, Nigeria's financial hub. When I got off the bus, the first thing that caught my eye was a sign that read, "Salesgirl Wanted Urgently. Apply in person."

"Ifeyinwa, be brave!" I muttered to myself as I walked into the big supermarket. I immediately landed my first job as a shop floor assistant, and this was the beginning of my success story, the first step in attaining the life I had dreamt of since reading the pages of my brothers' books.

In no time, my hard work caught the store owner's attention, who owned and managed a foundation for girls' education. Since then, I have enjoyed many open doors and opportunities, including a full scholarship to study Psychology at Georgetown University.

Ifeyinwa paused to look around the room. Then, she took a step back from the podium. Opening her arms wide, she said, "I am grateful for the things I could not control that worked out in my favour. I am grateful for the people who controlled things I could not control and ensured they worked out in my favour, and I am grateful for the things I had complete control over. Graduating class, your journey from here won't be linear but full of many twists and turns. Remember, you have the power to change the outcome of any circumstance, but first, you must understand that having a clear perspective of gratitude is the bedrock of success."

By now, there was absolute silence in the room. Ifenyinwa could feel the intensity of each person's emotional reaction to her speech. Some sniffled, some smiled, some looked overwhelmed, but one thing was sure: she could sense their hearts were full.

She ended her speech slowly as though counting her words. "What are you grateful for today?"

Prisoner of Guilt

Moshood Adebayo scrolled through an old article published on the PreventionWeb.net website. He moved his lips as he read the words on the screen but made no sound. Having memorised the details of the piece, he closed his laptop and walked away from his desk. He sat down on his custom-built, ergonomically designed rocking chair, confusion etched on his face. The chair, which had come highly recommended by his physiotherapist when he complained of frequent back pain due to long work hours, had become such a significant part of his life that he had it shipped to Bern before his arrival.

Gazing out at the beautiful landscape from his penthouse suite at the Hotel Allegro, Moshood reiterated what he had memorised: "The winter of 1999 was unusually severe in Switzerland, especially between January 27 and February 25. Over 5 metres of snow fell on the northern slopes of the Alps, more than the average total recorded in an entire winter. February saw a spate of avalanches throughout the Alps, causing extensive property damage and claiming many lives."

Having finished his recitation, he stood up and began to pace back and forth across the room. "It is now five years later, and it still feels like yesterday," he wailed. "I miss Amy! She shouldn't have. She shouldn't. The weather was not safe for skiing."

Returning to the desk, he reached for his journal and turned to a fresh page. "FEBRUARY 13, 2004!" he wrote in all caps. "Amy would have turned fifty years old today. This year feels better than last year. Even though I still feel torn, I am getting better at remembering how I would like to tell the story of Amy's passing."

Moshood put down his pen and reached for his wallet, where he kept Amy's picture. "I hate you, woman!" he yelled at the top of his lungs. As his breathing returned to normal, he ran his fingers through his thick, greying dreadlocks, straightened his black tie, perfectly shaped in a Van Wijk knot, adjusted his jacket, and headed down to the lobby.

"Hello, Mr Adebayo. My name is Ahmed, and I will be your driver for your stay. I understand you have a piece of furniture?"

"Oh, yes. It's my chair. I'll ask the hotel to get it for you. You are early. I have a quick meeting, and I should be ready in thirty minutes."

"That's fine, Mr Adebayo."

Moshood went to the hotel lobby to catch up with his old friend. Their annual coffee chat had become something they both looked forward to.

"Mosh, what's up, buddy? How are you holding up?" Matt asked.

"I am getting there. It's hard. I remember the details like they happened yesterday. Would you believe it's already five years? Hmmm. How is your wife—are you guys back together?"

"Oh, yeah, she never left. We had a rough few months, but all is looking up. I am so sorry for Amy. I remember the storms that night. Let me know if there's anything I can do to help. Maybe stay at ours instead of alone at the hotel next time you're here?"

"Thanks, Matt."

"Sometimes all you have to do is let it all out at once; that way, you speed up your healing process."

"Yeah, I have been trying to let it all out. I'll get there someday. I've got to go now, buddy."

After the brief reunion with Matt, Moshood got into the back seat of the cab.

"Tip?" the bellman asked after placing Moshood's chair in the trunk.

Moshood gave him ten Swiss Francs.

"Merci beaucoup," said the bellman with a bow.

"Hey! Turn up the heat," Moshood rudely instructed the cab driver.

"You could at least say that nicely; they already told me you're a difficult one," the driver muttered.

"What did you say?!" Moshood barked. But he did not wait for the man to reply. "Cab drivers are only necessary when my chauffeur is on vacation. Otherwise, you and I would never ride in a car together."

The driver took a few deep breaths to suppress his anger, and then, he cranked up the volume on the radio to drown Moshood out with an old jazz song.

"Turn that down; I can't hear myself think!" Moshood shouted.

The driver turned the music off.

"Down, not off," Moshood instructed.

Ahmed turned the radio back on and said, "Come on, man! You know you can control the volume from your seat, right? Enjoy!"

Moshood's phone rang.

"Hey Justin, I will be there in about two minutes—would've been faster if not for this moron of a driver."

"I don't think you deserve it, but keep the change anyways," Moshood said, tossing a wad of cash on the backseat when Ahmed pulled up to the front entrance of Schweizerhof.

Seated in the conference room, he heard Tanya say, "We will start by comparing actual to forecast for last year." But Moshood, restless, kept scrolling through pictures on his phone. It was a photo album of himself and Amy on one of their holidays to Switzerland, and coincidentally, he saw a picture of a dinner party they attended at the very same hotel where he and his colleagues were meeting. *Why do we have to meet here, of all places? Yes, Mr Bachmann is the president of Hemads Oil and Gas, but must he insist that we meet in Switzerland every year?!*

Moshood interrupted Tanya abruptly. "Sorry, Tanya, before you start, have you considered the new spending cut for our office in Birmingham? If we capture that accurately, we should have a twenty per cent savings in expenditure, and profit should increase by five per cent from last year." Giving Tanya no time to respond, he added, "I question your competence, Tanya. The least you could have done is have the financial report printed. A second grader knows to do just that!"

Everyone looked at him in bewilderment. Though Moshood often came off as arrogant and standoffish when he visited Switzerland, at home, in London, he was a different man entirely, one described by his colleagues as a true team player, supportive, kind, and thoughtful. His favourite colleague, Justin, pointed this out a few times, but Moshood blew off the remark. "This country angers me and excites me simultaneously," he offered.

"Sorry," he said timidly. "Excuse me, please." Moshood left the conference room. He followed the signs to the restroom, grabbed his phone, and called his doctor. "I am overwhelmed, doctor," he said frantically. "I feel unwell. Woozy. Like I am running out of breath."

"When did you notice these symptoms?"

"When I arrived in Bern two nights ago."

"Hmmm, you had the same symptoms when you were there last year. When are you back in London?"

"Friday night."

"Is your appetite normal?"

"I suppose so."

"And what was your last blood pressure reading?"

"It went up to 130/80 when I got here. I haven't checked today."

"You need to rest because of the light-headedness, but I won't recommend any medications. If you rest properly, your blood pressure should normalise. Send me your next reading.”

Feeling reassured, Moshood walked back into the conference room and sat beside Justin.

“Mike, I am eager to hear a rundown of our ongoing negotiation with Casablanca,” Mr Bachmann said.

Mike smiled. “Casablanca is looking good, and we should get approval from their head office in two weeks. Sam Ketel's only worry is that, erm, he thinks our budget is too steep. Jack Oil, K&O Oil Servicing Limited, and Kwaiti Oil and Gas are also bidding. Their budgets are about two to three million pounds.”

“Mike, you know we cannot afford to discount this,” Mr Bachmann said. He paused to take a sip of water, then looked at Moshood, who was getting out of his seat once again.

“We should not change our pricing,” Moshood agreed. “I’m sorry, I must leave now; I don’t feel well. I’ve just called my doctor, and he...”

“Ah! The annual knockout? Are you fit to fly back home tonight?” Mr Bachmann asked.

“I don’t know,” Moshood replied.

Mr Bachmann told the company’s Executive Assistant, “Emilia, get him a flight.”

"Sure! Aha! I found one for today! You'll arrive at Heathrow at 3 pm."

Moshood gave Emilia a thankful nod. "Could you also help get my chair back to London?"

"Sure! Anything else?"

"No."

Moshood thanked everyone for their support and returned to his hotel to pick up his luggage.

****

Moshood looked pale. He sipped the bottled water he had brought on the plane and signalled for a black cab at Heathrow Airport.

"SW10 0.. Yes, that one, house number 10," Moshood said as the cab driver entered his postcode into the GPS. I'll drop my luggage and head to Chelsea and Westminster Hospital."

As Moshood walked through the hospital doors, his eyes met the eyes of a nurse in the hallway. He gave her a half smile.

"It's unusually chilly out there, isn't it?" She asked. He smiled again, but he couldn't get himself to respond.

That lady reminds me of Amy. Wow! Look at those

cheekbones! He walked away quickly and went straight to Dr Zac's office.

"Your vitals look perfect. Blood pressure is 110/80 mm Hg, your breathing rate is 12 to 18 breaths per minute, and your temperature is 37.3°C."

"How can that be? When I landed at Heathrow, I felt lifeless."

"Let's follow up in two weeks and see if anything changes."

When he got home, Moshood lay on his couch and gazed at the ceiling. Tears welled up in his eyes and flowed freely when he could no longer hold them back. He rolled from the couch to his knees with his hands clasped together. "I am sorry, Amy," he repeated until the sun sank into oblivion and the early dark winter clouds covered the sky.

****

When Moshood returned to the office the following week, Justin asked, "Moshood, have you got five minutes?"

"Sure. I can talk for a bit now. What's up?"

"I heard Alphonse talking to Mr Bachmann. The report you submitted to the board contained too many errors. He is proposing you resign. You know he always has Mr Bachmann's ear."

"He is annoying! I called him the night I was putting the report together in Switzerland to tell him there was still some information to come, but this would not get in the way of the board making decisions about our strategic plans for next year. Now I know why Mr Bachmann wrote me a stinker." Moshood let out a loud sigh.

"Moshood, is there anything bothering you? I mean, you know, we are friends, and you can tell me anything. I have heard quite a few people gossiping about your work lately: the board report, the email you accidentally sent to Alex, and the transaction that cost us $25,000, which Mr Bachmann insists you pay because he reckons it was your negligence. You are one of the brightest guys on the leadership team and someone I look up to, but it seems you have been falling short for two weeks straight. What's up with you?"

Moshood sighed again. "It's just too much."

"Amy?" Justin asked.

"Well, yeah, erm, not really, I mean no."

"Sure about that?"

"Erm, maybe, but." Moshood choked on his words. "I don't know…. It's eating me up inside, Justin. It's just hard. My heart aches differently each time I remember her," Moshood confessed.

"Do you think seeing a therapist may help?"

"Hmm. Can of worms!" Moshood exhaled.

"Better to open it up sooner rather than later if you ask me," Justin said.

"Know anyone you can recommend?"

"Sure, I have seen one a few times. I will send you her number."

****

"Mr Adebayo or Moshood?"

"Moshood, thank you."

"Please take a seat." Dr Wilson smiled as she welcomed Moshood into her small but nicely ventilated office. "Thank you for your patience. The wait time on weekends is always longer."

"Oh, it's fine."

"So, this is your first time seeing a psychotherapist, right?" she asked.

"It is my first time, and I must confess that I'm a little nervous."

"Would you like some water or coffee?"

"Erm, water is fine."

Moshood gazed around the room as Dr Wilson retrieved

a cup from the side of her water cooler, filled it, and handed it to him.

"Thank you, Dr Wilson." He took a sip and placed it on the table to his left.

Dr Wilson adjusted her seat so she could speak to him face-to-face. "A psychotherapy session is just like having a conversation with someone you trust. You can share anything you'd like. It is a safe place to unburden yourself and soak in positive energy. The conversations may reveal some truth or make you revisit some incidents you'd rather forget, but the hope is that you find peace and freedom at the end."

"Sounds comforting," Moshood said. "But what if I don't want to share personal stories?"

"That is completely fine. You are under no obligation." Moshood looked at the exit sign over the door. "How long do we have?"

"As long as you are comfortable with continuing the conversation."

"Thank you," Moshood exclaimed, jumping to his feet. "I think we've reached the end of our first session. I am not ready. Can I please see you next week, Dr Wilson?"

"Next week is fine, Moshood."

****

"What brings you here today?" Dr Wilson asked Moshood as though their previous encounter had never happened.

"Well, first off, I'm ready. I've had to prepare mentally for today's session, but I'm ready now." He paused as if to consider her question. "I think my job is too demanding, and I would like our conversation to be about navigating the challenges while maintaining a positive mental outlook. You know?"

"Is it a new job?"

"No."

"Why is it so demanding? Has it always been this way? Or is this a recent development?" Dr Wilson asked.

"The deadlines are never-ending. To be fair, we work in a highly volatile sector."

"Do you think the deadlines are realistic? Who sets them?"

"No, they aren't. My boss, the CEO, and the board," Moshood huffed as he rolled his eyes."

"How long have you been working in this role?"

"A long time, some years."

"Do you find it challenging and motivating?"

"Yes, for sure. But equally daunting and stressful. I've had headaches for two weeks straight."

"Are you on any medication?"

"Yes, I take antidepressants and paracetamol for headaches. I have been self-medicating, and lately, I have been taking a sleeping pill every other night."

"Why do you need an antidepressant?"

Moshood got up abruptly, "Water, Dr Wilson?"

"Yes, thank you."

He sauntered to the water cooler, slowly filled two cups, and handed one to Dr Wilson. "Oops, I nearly spilled that," he said as he sat back in his seat.

"Was there a reason for the antidepressants?"

"To keep me alive. I guess. I feel like the world is caving in sometimes."

"How long have you had this feeling?"

"About five years."

"Do you remember any significant event that happened around that time?"

He looked away, his gaze fixed on the exit. "My wife, Amy." He lowered his head. "She died."

"I am so sorry to hear that," Dr Wilson said. "You must miss her terribly."

"Every day."

"And was it after her death that you started taking antidepressants?"

"Yes. I wasn't coping very well. Still not."

"What do you miss most about Amy?"

"Gosh, her smile. She had the most beautiful, captivating smile."

Dr Wilson smiled.

"And she had beautiful eyes. Amy was distinctively beautiful, Dr Wilson. I only wish I had told her so more often."

"Do you need a moment?"

"No. It is just hard to move on. I often have palpitations."

"When do you notice them?"

"Each time I think about Amy. It feels like my heart is going to explode. It tightens up, and it's hard to forgive myself."

"Forgive yourself? Was there something you did or think you should have done?"

"Oh, yes. If I had, I wouldn't be here today. Our marriage was imperfect from day one. I mean, we had heated arguments all the time, mostly because she had a terrible temper. She'd throw things, and I responded, triggered by her, with slaps and insults. It was unhealthy, but we survived and learned to live with each other with all the drama. We learned to love each other for the most part because we genuinely liked each other. Counselling helped in the early years.

Dr Wilson was quiet.

"I loved Amy—I did. I would do anything for her, but she betrayed me, and I cannot forgive her or myself. I am dying. Help me."

"Our souls are connected to our hearts, and our hearts are as healthy as our souls. I will help you," Dr Wilson said.

"Has this ever happened to you, Dr Wilson? You know the truth about a situation, but you lie to yourself for so long, for so many years, until the lie you tell yourself becomes your truth?"

"Like pretending something is not what it is?" Dr Wilson asked.

"Beyond pretending. My subconscious accepted the lie as truth."

"Even when we make mistakes, we can find hope in the frailty of our humanity and seek forgiveness. If the person from whom we seek forgiveness is no more, we can grant it on their behalf and forgive ourselves."

"I'm sorry, Dr Wilson. That sounds too spiritual for me."

Dr Wilson smiled. "Come with me," she said, leading him to the balcony. "Let's do a little exercise." She paused to open the doors. "The words we speak have the power to free us, heal us, or hold us captive and cage us. The choice is ours. Say after me, 'I will liberate myself with the truth today. I forgive myself for….'"

Moshood was quiet. He looked intently at the silhouette of the iconic London Eye against the dimming sky. Dr Wilson touched his shoulder gently. "Do you want to continue?"

"Yes. It happened in Switzerland."

"What did?"

"She died in Switzerland."

"Do you want to share more about Amy's death?"

"She and her friends had arranged a ski trip. It was not their first time, but it had been snowing heavily for days. I tried to talk her out of going. But there was no stopping her."

"Hmmm. So, you tried to stop Amy? You need to accept it's not your fault and release yourself from guilt, Moshood."

"She was buried under an avalanche in the Alps," he sniffed. "She was helpless."

"How did you hear about her death?"

"Like everyone else who lost a loved one that day, on the news."

"Oh, dear."

"If only I were more present and a little more compassionate and loving, I might have saved her. But I was in Spain on a business trip. Dr Wilson, I work hard."

Noticing him fidgeting, Dr Wilson stepped away from Moshood to give him space.

"I am sick and tired of taking medications to survive. Amy needs to get out of my head! She is draining the life out of me!"

Moshood realised he was speaking angrily and looked to the therapist for her response.

"Let's go back inside," she said, ushering him back to his seat.

"Dr Wilson, that was all a lie," Moshood confessed after Dr Wilson had shut the balcony doors. "That is the lie I've told myself and others all these years—the lie I have accepted to be the truth about Amy's death. Those details came from a news article that ran the night Amy died."

"What then is the truth, Moshood?" Dr Wilson asked softly. "The first step to finding forgiveness is acknowledging and accepting that you are wrong. This truth will heal and liberate you as you walk the journey of repentance."

Moshood took a deep breath. He leaned back into his chair. "We were in Switzerland holidaying, and she frequently chatted with a colleague. Mostly work stuff, but a few light-hearted conversations. The part that got me enraged was her text message when he mentioned he and his partner had been through some tough times. She said it was the same for her, that my toxic behaviour was becoming unbearable. She said she would leave me if we couldn't work things out. Her colleague responded with a smiley face and a heart, offering a listening ear if she needed to talk, and Amy thanked him with a heart and a hug emoji. I was enraged, and without thinking, I hit her head with a vase. Horrified by what I'd done and how much blood she was losing, I rushed her to the hospital. I told the doctors she fell in the bathroom at our hotel. She was unconscious for weeks before passing away, so she could not challenge my version of events."

"You…you what?" Dr Wilson stuttered, white-faced.

"Yes, Dr Wilson, I accidentally killed my beloved Amy," Moshood sobbed. "I shouldn't have," he said, bitter tears streaming down his face and into his mouth. "I overreacted."

Slowly, discreetly, Dr Wilson reached for the emergency buzzer under her desk. She tried not to show her fear or discomfort while Moshood rambled on and on about how free he felt now that he'd spoken the truth out loud and about how right she'd been in leading him through that exercise. She simply nodded and waited, hoping he would not jump out of his seat and leave as he'd done during their first session.

Within minutes, the police stormed Dr Wilson's office, handcuffed Moshood, and led him out to their patrol car as he cried out, "It was an accident. I am not a dangerous man. Dr Wilson, can you help me find forgiveness?"

Miracles Everywhere!

The 8.45 pm train from Canning Town to London City Airport was late. Pastor Joshua Komolafe JP, affectionately called PJ by his congregants, stood behind the yellow safety line at the platform's edge but close enough to see an approaching train come out of the tunnel. His eyes were fixed on the electronic screen flashing arrival and departure updates. The next DLR train should be the one to take him to London City Airport.

He moved closer to the screen and squinted as he tried to read the latest updates but was distracted by a young, mixed-race woman of medium height and build, dressed in distressed blue skinny jeans and a burnt-orange-and-gold sleeveless top, staggering around the platform. Bumping into him, she swept her hair to the left, revealing a fading pink heart tattoo on her neck. The black border line around the heart was thin and broken. She smiled at him from the corner of her mouth and yelled, "It isn't coming until 9.30!" She chewed the gum in her mouth to the rhythm of the Jubilee line train approaching on the opposite side of the platform.

He looked at her for a second, smiled, and then looked at the information display again. "9.30! Dear me!" PJ yelled out as the information board updated itself.

"You may want to find another route, darling, and when you

do, you better take me with you."

"I reject temptation. Take you with me? Seriously?" he muttered to himself. He looked at the girl from the corner of his eye, hissed, then made a military turn and ran down the escalators. "Excuse me, please!" he cried out, pushing past other commuters who casually held onto the handrail in no rush at all.

A group of teenagers obstructed his path, running down and back up again against the escalator's descending movement. PJ leaned into the tall, skinny one standing directly before him. "Excuse me, please," he said calmly and softly. Then he turned to the one blocking him on the right and repeated his request.

The teenagers ignored him. The one in front of him giggled when he noticed PJ's flared nostrils, curled lips and creased forehead.

"Yo! Mason, the train is coming, mate. Are we going to Westfield?"

PJ squeezed past the two boys, making sure to elbow the one on his left. "Sorry," he said—though he was not—when the wheel of his hand luggage landed on the other boy's toe.

The guy closed in on PJ and bumped into him with his chest. "Beat him up!" he called to his friends.

"Omar, leave it, man," one told him. "The train is here."

PJ remained unperturbed as the boys walked away from the scene. In his imagination, he had beaten them black and blue. However, the words of Matthew 5:9, "Blessed are the peacemakers, for they shall be called the sons of God," echoed in his head and gripped his heart, preventing him from actually raising his fists when Omar tried to pick a fight. He clutched the 24-carat cross pendant that sat on his moderately protruding belly. "Father, forgive me," he prayed. "I missed a moment to share your love with those boys."

He googled alternate directions to London City Airport. The fastest option was to catch a bus from Hermit Road. He tried to run through the exit, but the tyres of his hand luggage got trapped between the closing barriers. He manoeuvred it angrily, freeing it from the gates' claws. Regaining his composure, he exhaled. *I am going to do the work of the Lord. I don't need all these distractions at all. I don't.*

He made the sign of the cross as he walked briskly towards Hermit Road. "Jesus, I need your help," he whispered.

"I've always wondered what Christianity truly means," the young lady he'd encountered on the DLR platform said. "Never got an answer to my many questions." She picked up her pace to keep up with him.

"Oh! Hello." PJ paused as if contemplating how to introduce himself. "My name is Pastor Joshua Komolafe JP. I don't like to put the title out there too often, but yeah, I can help you find the answers you seek." He smiled. "I can chat for a few minutes before the bus arrives. My job is to lead people to the Truth. What do you want to know?"

She shrugged and continued slowly. "My mum is chronically depressed, my dad is an unrepentant alcoholic, and living at home is literally hell. I live on the streets when I can't find anyone to take me in. Life is just too hard, and I can't cope anymore. I need answers, and I am running out of time."

PJ reached into his pockets. "I usually have Christian literature handy for curious minds like yours," he explained. "I am so sorry. It has answers to-to-to…"

"Who is Jesus, and what does He mean to you?" she asked.

His phone rang, interrupting their conversation. "Yes, yes. Yes," he said, motioning to her to hold on for one moment before ending his call abruptly. "I'll tell you what: Oh, the bus is here. I have a flight to catch—I'm going to Budapest to preach at my friend's new mega-church, but why don't you connect with me on Instagram? I can reach out as soon as I'm back. It's @PJ-JP."

"Cool. I'm Olivia, but you can call me Liv. I'm following you now."

"It's Great to meet you, Liv! I'll reach out soon!" he said as the bus driver closed the doors.

****

"Welcome back, Pastor. How was your trip?" asked Ade as he took PJ's bags and followed him into his small office at the back of the foyer.

"Who is leading the opening exhortation for today's midweek service?" PJ asked, ignoring his assistant's question.

"Patricia."

"Why Patricia?"

"Pastor Anna asked me to look for an alternative. She said David was, erm…"

PJ pounded his fist on the table. "She said what?" PJ gave Ade the once over. "Your shoelaces are not properly tied, and your trousers are starting to unravel at the edges. Fix it!" He paused, then repeated his question. "Why isn't Pastor Anna here? Why would my wife send my staff a text? I should be the first to know. Don't you think, Ade?"

Embarrassed, Ade simply nodded. "Pastor Anna said Cristina could not work this evening. She has no one to look after David. She said she left you a voicemail but texted me just in case you didn't hear it in time."

"That is the problem I have with her. She needs to be more supportive. Son, make sure you marry a woman who supports you no matter what. Look at me! I work hard. I work very hard," PJ said, using his baritone preaching voice. "I came here straight from the airport to preach the midweek service. That is passion, son; I am intoxicated by the Gospel. We must do the work of the Lord. The church must grow!" He clapped his hands several times. He did that whenever he was excited or talking about church growth.

He opened his hand luggage and reached for a bottle of water. After a few sips, he said softly but reassuringly, "The revival in Budapest was incredibly powerful!"

"That's awesome," Ade said.

"Hallelujah! Hallelujah! Hallelujah!" He waved his hands in the air with each repetition of the word. "Before I forget," he said, "please make sure all the church leaders meet me immediately after the closing prayer. There are so many lessons to share from my trip." He smiled. "I would also like to meet with you and Nathan. I hear you couldn't get along in my absence."

"Sure, PJ," Ade nodded.

****

As soon as PJ stepped into their three-bedroom, semi detached house, he heard sobs. He put his hand luggage in his home office and went upstairs to the living room, where he found his wife on the sofa, her face cupped in her hands, her yellow flowery dress damp from her tears.

"Anna, how are you? How is David?" PJ asked.

"Worse! David is getting weaker, Josh," she sobbed. "I am drained and completely void of hope." She wiped her tears with the back of her hands. "Did we offend God?"

"What do you mean?" PJ asked. He walked toward David's room without giving Anna a chance to respond.

"Don't wake him up! He only fell asleep thirty minutes ago, and it was a struggle."

PJ turned to face his wife. "No, we did not offend God, and I don't think crying will solve anything. The boy will be fine. I think we should hire a second caregiver. That way, you can have more time to relax in the evenings, and all the tension and frustration will disappear." He sat down at the piano bench to take off his shoes. "Pastor Yomi's wife sends her love," he said, changing the subject. "Budapest was electrifying, Anna. He paused briefly, then changed tracks. "I met with our leaders after today's service to discuss how we can grow our church rapidly like Pastor Yomi. Nathan suggested we get a loan, move to a bigger building in Stratford and change our name from Peaceful Community Church to something catchy like Miracle Church for All Nations! We even came up with a plan to grow the church to five hundred members in eight months." He slid his hands across the piano keys, hoping the soothing melody would ease the sadness filling the room. "And the church said… Amen!"

PJ looked to his wife, trying to gauge her enthusiasm, but Anna simply sighed in exasperation. "Is that all you have to say, Joshua?!" she cried, raising her head to meet his gaze. "David is turning thirteen tomorrow—thirteen! And he doesn't even know it's his birthday. Our son is dying right before our eyes, and your only concern is growing the church. Really, Joshua? Ah! You are a selfish man! You have literally abandoned David—you spend ninety per cent of your time away from your family, yet you claim to be a pious man, a servant of the Lord. You don't care about us as much as you care about raising your profile amongst your pastor friends. And to what end? Tell me!"

A deafening silence fell over the room as PJ sat in

disbelief.

"David is my priority," Anna whispered as she rose from her seat. "You do as you wish!" She marched out of the living room and slammed the door.

"It was never like this," he said quietly, looking skyward. "We loved each other—I don't know why we drifted apart. Honestly, I can't bear the burden of having to see David in such excruciating pain. Church is my only escape. Please, God, heal him—please heal him. Only you can. This pain is just too much to bear."

Scrolling through his texts, he found a message Anna had sent him three months earlier, complaining bitterly about his abysmal behaviour toward her and how he had become short-fused. She had even asked him to attend counselling several times, but PJ had declined, claiming he had conflicting meetings. "She is right, but I know nothing else can bring absolute peace back into our marriage if David isn't healed. God, please heal David. I know you can. I believe."

Satisfied that God had heard and would answer his prayer, PJ tiptoed into his son's room and gently laid his hands on David's chest. "Each heartbeat is a gift from God," he whispered to the sleeping boy, "and He will keep it going, not in pain and sorrow, but in good health. God will heal you, David. I still believe, even in my darkest moments, I still believe all will be well."

****

"PJ, our new home will soon be the talk of the town," Nathan proclaimed as the men admired the modern, beautifully appointed, five-hundred-seat facility they acquired in Stratford. "I am pleased we can finally be more impactful. Miracle Church for All Nations marks the beginning of a new dawn."

Ade interrupted their conversation before PJ could assent. "Pastor, five people would like you to pray for them."

"Please show them in. Nathan, don't go—we need to continue our conversation after this and Ade, you should join us."

Nathan stood at the entrance of PJ's office as the pastor prayed for the beleaguered congregants—two with severe migraines that wouldn't go away and a young man who sought encouragement because he was having a tough time at work.

"Social media and word of mouth are probably the main reasons we had such a good turnout today," Nathan said enthusiastically as the last congregant walked away. "But I think we need to do even more. I think we should target at least three hundred new members over the next two months.”

“Two months? How do we achieve that?” PJ asked. “Have you forgotten we started this church on January 1, 2016? That was only eight months ago! Three hundred new members in two months is definitely an unattainable goal! We must start planning community events as soon as possible!” He said.

PJ turned to Ade, who was taking the meeting minutes, and waited for him to look up from his iPad. “Ade, I want to hear your views, too,” he said encouragingly.

“We are in the business of problem-solving,” Nathan continued as if PJ had not just requested Ade’s input. “If we meet their needs, the people will keep coming to us. I’ll give you an example. PJ, you just prayed for those two poor souls with migraines, but nothing happened. They left just as they came—in pain. Maybe they’ll get better later, I don’t know. But imagine if you prayed for them during the service and their healing began instantly.”

“Sorry, Nathan, if I may,” Ade cut in. “God is the healer; we cannot question His sovereignty if one gets healed and another doesn’t. Sometimes, we don’t have all the answers, but we keep hoping and believing. So, what happens if PJ prays for someone’s healing and nothing happens?”

"That's theology, and I know you went to Bible school and all that, but miracles can be engineered," Nathan countered. "I have seen it."

PJ's mind drifted back to the days, weeks, and months he and Pastor Anna had spent crying their eyes out and praying, begging God to heal David. Yet, David was still not out of the woods five years later. In fact, his condition, Duchenne Muscular Dystrophy, a rare and incurable genetic disorder which made it impossible for him to move his arms and legs, continued to deteriorate, making it difficult for him to even sit upright in his wheelchair and causing him to scream out in distress.

"Engineered? Nathan, come on! You can't be for real!?" Ade said.

"PJ," Nathan said, "I think we should try it out next week."

"Try what out?" PJ asked, jolted from his reverie.

"Engineered miracles."

PJ laughed. "Nathan, what are you talking about?"

"Trust me on this. Each week, we plant at least three actors among the members of our church and have you lay your hands on them and pray. Then, after prayers, you would make an announcement, asking anyone who has felt their symptoms dissipate or disappear to share their story. We can write a script for them."

"I think we should consult all the church leaders before making a decision," Ade said, making little effort to hide his opposition to Nathan's scheme.

"Look, Ade, this is the leadership right here." Nathan pointed at PJ. "If he says yes, we don't need anyone else's approval."

"Have you prayed about it?" Ade asked.

Nathan uncrossed his legs. "We have hundreds of thousands of pounds of loan to repay, and money still doesn't grow on trees," he said, raising his voice angrily as he looked Ade in the eyes. "We need to pluck it out of people's pockets. How? We meet a need, and we get rewarded for it. As the Head of Operations of this church, I am responsible for ensuring we don't go out of business. Got it?"

Ade placed his iPad on PJ's mahogany table. "That is deception! Don't be like Judas, whom the devil tempted because of his love for money."

PJ reached for the remote control of his sound system and lowered the volume on the beautiful worship instrumental playing in the background. "Gentlemen, don't let your tempers flare up," he cautioned. "Let us reason together and not criticise one another." He looked to his assistant. "There's no need to be judgmental, Ade. My motivation for becoming a Pastor has not changed after all these years. It's all about impact, positive, transformational impact, but how do you become impactful without growth? God won't come down and teach us how to grow our church; we need to figure that out ourselves. I have so many friends who started their churches after us, and they are doing very well. Some have congregations numbering in the thousands, one just bought his second private jet, and countless charities serve the various needs of their communities. It is all about making the greatest impact possible, but, of course, we must be careful in how we achieve our goals."

Ade sighed in defeat. "Pastor," he said, his voice shaky yet resolute, "if you do this, I will have to resign as your assistant. I am not looking to be a goody two shoes here or claiming to be the most pious among us, but this plan goes against my beliefs –and I cannot compromise those." He paused for a minute as if choosing his next words carefully. "How about we share our salvation stories and trust God's transformative power to heal, deliver, and save the people? I'll go first. PJ picked me up off the streets of Leytonstone. I had nothing—no job, no ambition, no future, and no hope. I felt empty—I knew there was more to life, but there was a vacuum in my soul that nothing could fill. Trust me, I tried everything. I remember I was particularly sombre that day from excessive drinking. But as PJ shared the Word with me, I felt an inexplicable peace. It was as if Psalm 46:1-3, which says that God is our refuge and strength, an ever present help in trouble, were the antidote to my empty soul."

"You have shared this story before," Nathan said dismissively.

But Ade ignored him and forged ahead. "From that day on, I wanted to hear more of what PJ said. I can proudly say I am now a child of God, and it is all by His Grace. There is nothing I did to deserve His boundless love."

PJ smiled. "I remember that day," he said.

"How many people have decided to become Christians because of your salvation story, Ade?" Nathan asked.

"When Peter spoke in the book of Acts, three thousand people were added to the church in one day. How many have come to believe because of your story?"

Ade threw his hands up in the air. "God's power is always available to save—it's not so much about the story I, or anyone else, shares—it is about the power behind the transformation, which comes from within."

PJ cranked the music back up and grabbed a can of Coca-Cola from the mini fridge in the corner of his office. "Care for one?" he asked his colleagues.

Nathan and Ade chorused, "No. Thanks."

"PJ, why aren't you saying anything?" Nathan asked.

He sipped his drink, then rested his elbows on his desk. "What you are suggesting requires deep reflection, Nathan. Hmmm. Budapest was an eye-opening trip. Pastor Yomi's congregation is not even two years old, and they just moved to this dope auditorium that seats one thousand; they run four services on Sundays and plan to open a branch in Africa next year, and all the A-list preachers from the United States grace their podium. Pastor Yomi is one of the richest pastors in Budapest, no kidding."

Ade tapped his fingers on his lap rhythmically. "May I, please?" he asked. "Pastor, our mission is to introduce people to the transforming power of Christ. I think there is a distortion here. Are we competing with other pastors, or do we all share this same goal? What's the race to run four services when the motive is self-gratification? Are we a commercial organisation now? I am sorry, but this doesn't sound right. And, if I can be brutally honest, Nathan, you got it wrong! Our expansion to Stratford was not God-inspired!"

PJ stood up abruptly. "Enough, Ade! Enough!"

Nathan stood and put his arm around PJ. "It's okay, PJ.

Don't get all worked up."

"Get out of my office!" PJ shouted, showing Ade the door.

"I am sorry, PJ. I didn't mean to."

"I said, get out!" PJ ordered.

As soon as Ade walked out, Nathan asked, "Should I go ahead with the plan? I can get three actors for this weekend. We will have to pay them, though. Hundred pounds each per appearance. The church's growth is significant to me, PJ. We will give it a big push on social media."

"We should be careful," he said, sitting back in his chair. He took a deep breath and looked Nathan straight in the eye. "What about David?" he asked slowly, his pain audible.

"David? What about him?"

"What if the people find out? How do we explain that our church, Miracle Church for All Nations, is where unbelievable miracles happen, yet my son hasn't been— can't be—cured? It just doesn't make sense, Nathan. Sometimes, I feel my life contradicts the Gospel of faith."

"PJ, I understand and share your pain," Nathan said softly. "But we just cannot do church on a small scale. I remember the vision you shared with me a few years ago. You said you saw yourself preaching to a huge crowd of people. We are now on the right path, PJ. Thanks to your hard work and commitment, that dream is about to come true. It's harvest time, PJ. You could be the richest pastor in London."

PJ placed the empty can of Coca-Cola on the cocktail table next to him. He sighed deeply. "Okay, Nathan. You have my approval. But please keep this plan between us."

"What about Ade?"

"Leave him out of it." His mind wandered as he clutched the 24-carat gold cross pendant around his neck. Returning to the moment just as quickly as he'd left it, he looked at Nathan. "Let's bring this meeting to a close with a prayer; would you like to pray us out?"

"Yes," Nathan said as he bowed his head while PJ knelt on the ground. "Father, we are all sinners. Forgive us. Ade crossed the line today, but I forgive him. Thank You for giving me the wisdom to grow this church. We are excited and thank You for the strength and courage to be among the chosen few who bear Your torch of hope in this dark, dark world. We pray in Your name. Amen."

****

"Lift up your hands and ask God for anything," PJ told the assembled crowd of about one hundred and eighty, using his baritone preaching voice and waving his hands slowly and steadily. "There's an undeniable healing power in this place today." His eyes caught Nathan's gaze as he spoke these words, and Nathan winked at him. "I invite you to join me on the stage if you are sick and need to be prayed for."

At first, no one responded. Looking around, Nathan noticed two of the actors he'd hired were no longer seated. Panicked, he hastily took his phone out of his pocket. It slid out of his hands onto the floor, causing the screen to crack. Bending down to retrieve it, he saw the women re-enter the auditorium.

"You almost missed it," he hissed.

"We went to the restroom," they chorused.

"You're up—now. Go!"

The ladies ran to the stage just as PJ recited a prayer over the third actor, a young man who claimed to have a sharp pain in his knee. "I am healed!" the man suddenly shouted. "It's been there all week, the pain. But as you prayed, Pastor, I felt a sensation run through my legs, and it's completely gone!"

Bewilderment filled the auditorium, and the congregants applauded in awe as the young man ran around the room in excitement. One church member in the front row even shed a few tears. Nathan read her lips: "This is just too awesome," she said.

Then, the two women shared their stories. One said she had a migraine; the other, terrible abdominal pain. And both swore that their pain dissipated as soon as PJ laid his hands on them. "The pain moved from my stomach to my thighs, then to my legs and feet, and, just like that, it was gone," insisted the shapely older actress who had midnight-black hair and a pink scarf around her neck. When she smiled, her oyster-white teeth lit up the room.

"Hallelujah!" PJ clapped. "Miracles happen here!!! You should invite all your friends and family to church." His baritone preaching voice masked the tension in his voice.

****

"Hello, Nathan. Can you hear me?" PJ cleared his throat. "I've got bad news: Ade resigned!"

"I may sound cold, PJ, but that's not bad news. He was a stumbling block. The Bible says we need to speak to our mountains and ask them to move. Ade was a mountain."

"You are being insensitive, Nathan."

"I'm sorry, PJ, but just look at the account balance. Donations are pouring in, and we are well-positioned to pay off our loan early. This will allow us to do much more than we'd initially planned."

"I must confess, I feel bad. Ade has been with me for so many years, you know. He looked up to me as a mentor, and I feel I failed him."

"What does Ade know about church business? Nothing! We have done nothing wrong; we used our God-given intellect to move God's mission forward. Where is the sin?"

"So, what next? Are we going to produce more miracles?"

"Oh, yes! We can't stop now. The social media guys have great content from yesterday's service. The miracles were glorious!"

****

Sunday, November 17th, 2018, will go down in the history of the collective Christian community in London as the day the most wonder-provoking event ever occurred.

The choir looked extra fabulous that morning. The ushering team was aligned on the aisle, coordinated in colourful blazers and black trousers. PJ had instructed Nathan to double-check everything from the sound system to the cleanliness of the restrooms; everything had to be perfect because they were welcoming their first guest preacher, Apostle Kojo Frimpong, from Ghana. PJ couldn't believe the Apostle had accepted the invitation to preach at Miracle Church for All Nations. It only took one email and phone call, and he said yes.

"Thank you, Jesus," Apostle Kojo exclaimed as he stepped onto the stage and knelt behind the podium. "Thank you." Then he stood up and started singing. "I see miracles everywhere. The Glory is in this place. God is here to heal today. Sing with me, choir."

The choir was all too happy to join in. It was a song they knew well.

"Sing it softly now," Apostle Kojo instructed them, closing his eyes tightly and gradually opening them. "I sense God is about to do something remarkable here today. Stepping off the stage, he approached PJ and Pastor Anna. "Do you have a son?" he asked them.

"Yes!" Pastor Anna answered.

Apostle Kojo closed his eyes again. "That's interesting. PJ has never mentioned him. But I can see him. He is getting up from a wheelchair. The power of God is strengthening his arms and legs. I see a miracle happening in his spine. The power of God is touching him right now. Sing louder, choir, sing. Is anyone here sick? Believe, and you will receive healing."

Nathan, who was behind PJ, looked at him quizzically. "Did you engineer this?" he whispered in PJ's ear.

"Me?! I don't know what's going on. You are in charge of the actors."

"I did not hire any for today since you weren't preaching," Nathan said.

"Where is the boy?" Apostle Kojo asked Pastor Anna.

"He is… he is in my…"

"Apostle, please don't call on him," PJ interjected; "it is not possible for him to be healed."

Suddenly, there was an uproar from the back of the church. David, who typically watched the service from the monitor in his mother's office, was making his way, one baby step at a time, towards the stage, his caregiver following behind while screaming.

"What happened to the boy?" Apostle Kojo asked Cristina, handing her the microphone for all to hear.

"The minute you started singing, he lifted his head and looked at the screen," Cristina said, her hands shaking. "Then I heard a crack and pop, and, miraculously, he put his right foot down on the ground, then the left, and he got up slowly, using his hands to lift himself out of the wheelchair.

He told me he felt a flash of power, like an electric current running through his body. I have never seen anything like this!"

Pastor Anna ran to David and threw her arms around him. She was sobbing uncontrollably.

"Mum, I can't believe it, David exclaimed. "It's beyond me how this can happen. Look at me, Mum," he said, raising his arms and kicking his legs. "No pain!"

Nathan looked on in bewilderment as PJ fell to his knees, raised his hands toward Heaven, and screamed, "Thank you, God. Thank you!" Then he got up, walked over to his son, and lifted him off his feet. He kept thanking God as he carried him to the stage.

"David, would you tell the church what happened?" Apostle Kojo asked.

"All I can say is I have a new body," he giggled. "It's a dream come true—or is it a dream?! Like, is this actually happening to me right now?"

"Oh, what joy. Thank you, God!" Apostle Kojo echoed PJ. "Sing louder, choir, sing louder. Is anyone here sick? Miracles are happening here today. The Miracle Worker is here!" he cried out fervently.

Wailing filled the room, and the more the choir sang, the more miracles occurred. A wave of recovery swept through the crowd, and many were recorded to have received divine healing that could only be described as miraculous.

From the corner of his eye, PJ saw Nathan get up from his seat, his arms folded across his chest, his face pensive, like he was questioning what had just happened. Their eyes met briefly, then Nathan shrugged and left the auditorium with his head bowed.

The Apostle gave PJ the microphone. "Miracles still happen," he proclaimed, breaking down. "Hallelujah!" After what had just transpired, PJ concluded that preaching was unnecessary. Instead, he had David run the stage length, hugged him again, and brought the service to a close.

****

"Have you read the *Metro* yet?" Luke, who had replaced Ade, asked when PJ had answered his mobile phone.

"No. Why? Any exciting news about the church?"

"I think it's best if you see it yourself," Luke said hesitantly. "We are in big trouble,".

"Trouble? What for? Did Nathan say anything? He is the only one who handles PR, but he's been away on vacation since David's healing last week. I'll call you back—I'm almost at the station—I'll pick up a copy."

Pushing past the morning commuters, PJ ran to the nearest paper stand and grabbed a copy of the local paper. "Miracle Church for All Nations is a scam!" read the front page headline. Senior Pastor Joshua Komolafe is a fake. Members beware!"

PJ could not believe his eyes. Nathan had written a tell all account of how he and PJ had deceived people into believing PJ had the power to heal. He admitted that they had actors on the payroll who faked receiving miracles and said he was ashamed to have participated in such a dubious, disgraceful and duplicitous role after he witnessed the real miracle of David's healing. Nathan apologised for masterminding the deception, insisting he had good intentions in wanting to grow the church.

"Nathan, why, why would you do this?"

Returning home, he called Nathan many times to ask him this very question, but his phone went straight to voicemail each time. So, he turned to God instead. "I am sorry, Father. It's all my fault. I got carried away by all the accolades and the prestige. Vanity, it's all vanity. I am so sorry. Jesus, please have mercy on me." He said as bitter tears flowed down his face. With a sorrow-bowed head, he prayed, "Forgive me, please, please forgive me."

Suddenly, he got a notification on his phone. It was an

Instagram message.

"This is Liv. I met you at Canning Town some years ago. I am still searching for answers. Pray for me?"

PJ cried even louder as his knees hit the floor. With arms high in total surrender, he whispered, "Please, give me a second chance."

PLEASE, DON'T CALL ME A POET.

Poetry is the truest form of conversation with your soul. And I have become a generous soul, giving back to the world the words divinely planted in me.

Exhale

I've been broken,
I've been bruised.
Dejected and,
Twice rejected.

I've been beaten,
I've been mocked,
Abandoned,
Thrice handcuffed.

In pain, I learned peace.
In tribulations, trust,
In hope, patience,
In sorrow, joy.

In everything, I learned to exhale.

Mon Ami

Like hands that fit into a glove,
Like the clouds that canopy the sky,
Like pink roses from Hyde Park Garden,
Like Häagen-Dazs on a summer afternoon,
You are a perfect reflection of what friendship should be.

Speak up!

Handicapped by society's stereotypes,
Detained for living my truth.
Incarcerated by the people who define freedom of speech,
Cowards who speak in their basements but never on the
mountaintop.
Hypocrites who favour only those having sufficient substance to
keep them in power.

"Speak!" they said.
Everyman may use the air in his lungs as he wishes.
"Speak!" they said.

Yet they counted my words,
They listened to every syllable.
They listened to weigh my bravery on their perverted scales.
They listened to trap me, twist my words, and silence me completely.
They listened to recount my accusation of the ills they have caused
the common man.

They listened.
They listened.

Oh, but where can I find a righteous judge?

Do not despair

Do not despair
When destiny delays
The dreams of your heart
Do not despair.

Do not despair
When destiny defers
The longings of your heart
Do not despair.

During this period of temporary defeat,
Your inner man will destroy death traps along your path.
And you will become stronger in the waiting,
Do not despair.

Ease my burden

What makes life worth living?
To wake up each morning and chase after a shadow?
A shadow that exists in bodily form, tangible but inconsequential.
What makes life worth living?

Humanity's longing to be a people united to chase the woes of poverty away from the high streets of gold is only a dream. The individualism of their dreams preoccupies each of them. They pretend, choosing not to hear the strain in the voices of their brothers and sisters in need.

Benevolent and merciful One, haven't you taught us that the way of life is love? To hold our neighbour's tired hands and bear each other's burdens. For who truly has ascended without your mercy upon him? These humans hold on tightly to your loving-kindness and tender mercies, which they have received in abundance.

But today, I come as one of those humans, seeking my portion for the fattening of my soul. I come without pretences, asking for the quota reserved for kings. For what does it matter if my barns are empty and my heart is full of good that I know not how to give?

I come as one of them. But I ask for your strength so I do not end up in the ocean of emptiness reserved for those who held on tightly to what they freely received.

It's already a thousand years—please ease my burden!

People Palava

Some people are hard to love.
Nothing you do will satisfy them,
Nothing you say will brighten their day.

Some people are hard to please.
Counting mistakes each time you fail,
Shifting the blame and passing the guilt.

Some people are human.
Nothing they do should bother you,
Nothing they say should shatter you.

It's all people palava!

Destiny Dances

Destiny dances
around the fire of nonchalance.

Time passes
circling the planet seven times.

Remembering death is inevitable
they lose hope.

Accepting the common man's disease,
they set sail. To a place where no one returns.

They decay.
They decay.

Until they are emptied
of their power to desire.

I Miss You

Staring through memory-stained windows,
It is hard to forget the love we once shared.
In your eyes, I saw hope for tomorrow,
In every sense, you were my hero.

Trying to move on like these zooming cars,
Time would never heal my hidden scars.
I'm all alone in this empty house,
And your voice echoes through the red brick walls.

Breathing your last was painful to watch,
But letting you go was heaven's embrace.
Even in grief, there'll be moments of relief,
Even in tears, there'll be moments of joy.

Nap

Silence crawled into my room,
Asking us to be friends.
The 6.45 am train to Barking Town interrupts her 100th plea.

Boredom knocked louder today.
There were so many cracks in my door.
But to my surprise, the knocks faded away too soon.

Deception filled the atmosphere.
With a loud cheer, I jumped to my feet,
And danced without beats.

Consciousness introduced me to reality.
And I woke up from my sleep.
It was meant to be a nap.

Honestly, it was meant to be a nap.

Unmask the pretenders

Hands up above my head, up above my heart.
My soul awakened to the thoughts of finally finding a home.
Immersed in honest service, oblivious to selfish ambition.
Shadowed by purity, ignorant to the wiles of humanity.

Unity is destroyed by individualism.
Puppet followers desire the master's cloak.
The deceit of flowery talk entangles the unaware, the unintentionally
ignorant.
Who assemble weekly for their daily supply of strength.

Is there no place to call home?
Where love, the non-self-seeking, non-vainglorious kind of love, is
the reason for our gathering.
Fragile souls cry out in anguish.
But on the seventh, they'll gather again to be torn into pieces.

Hands clasped in penitence, I'm lost in the intensity of the knowledge
of One.
I offer my soul, my heart, my sweet service.
Boundless love, fearless love, holds me steady, keeps me strong.
I've finally found a home not made of bricks and mortar.

Switch

At the intersection of night and day,
The firmament observes in silence.
As the moon gives way for the sun to rise,
Daffodils tingle at the glimpse of the morning.
My brewing coffee, the Kenyan roast, intoxicates me again.
Life is unfolding as it should, as it should.

Herbs for my wound

You greeted me with wide eyes,
You welcomed me with arms apart.
You invited me to dine with you,
You comforted me with bread and soup.

I felt at home. I felt secure.
Your kindness and your warmth were a blanket for my soul.
But just when I thought I had found solace in you,
You stabbed me in the back, then gave me herbs for my wound.

Illusions

One day, you will realise worries are just illusions.
That's what they are meant to be. Nothing more than illusions.
But you give them life.

You take each worrying thought and stretch it out across the length
of your life.
Forgetting each worry has no power to live except the power you
give to it.

"How did I get so many wrinkles?" You ask again.

Illusions, my friend. Your wrinkles are illusions.

The Path

There is a reason for all of life's journeys.
And for every reason, there is a season.
And for every season, a beautiful beginning.